DISGUSTING PLANTS

BY PATRICK PERISH

EPIC

BELLWETHER MEDIA • MINNEAPOLIS, MN

EPIC

EPIC BOOKS are no ordinary books. They burst with intense action, high-speed heroics, and shadows of the unknown. Are you ready for an Epic adventure?

This edition first published in 2015 by Bellwether Media, Inc.

Library of Congress Cataloging-in-Publication Data

Perish, Patrick, author.
Disgusting Plants / by Patrick Perish.
pages cm. – (Epic. Totally Disgusting)
Summary: "Engaging images accompany information about disgusting plants. The combination of high-interest subject matter and light text is intended for students in grades 2 through 7"– Provided by publisher.
Audience: Ages 7-12.
Audience: Grades 2 to 7.
Includes bibliographical references and index.
ISBN 978-1-62617-132-9 (hardcover : alk. paper)
ISBN 978-0-531-27224-4 (paperback : alk. paper)
1. Plants–Miscellanea–Juvenile literature. I. Title.
QK49.P47 2014
580–dc23
2014008258

Printed in the United States of America, North Mankato, MN.

TABLE OF CONTENTS

TOTALLY GROSS GREENS!

Not all plants are pretty like sunflowers and daisies. Some plants smell like **rotting** meat. Others can even eat small animals. These gross greens will not be in your mom's garden.

NOT SO SWEET SCENTS

Sometimes it is nice to stop and smell the flowers. However, you might want to skip the skunk cabbage. This swamp plant can warm itself. It heats up to spread its rotten egg **odor**.

Sort of Disgusting
Totally Disgusting
GROSS-O-METER

Sort of Disgusting
Totally Disgusting
GROSS-O-METER

The jackal food plant is a **parasite** on other plants. Its flowers come out of the ground after heavy rainfall. Then it releases an awful stink. The smell is so bad it attracts **dung** beetles!

BAD NEIGHBORS

This creep lives by latching onto nearby plants. It sucks their juices out through the roots.

Rafflesia is another parasite. It is called the meat flower because it smells like **carrion**. Its stench attracts flies looking for rotten flesh.

BIG STINK

Rafflesia **has the largest flower in the world. It can grow up to 3 feet (1 meter) across. It can weigh up to 15 pounds (7 kilograms)!**

Sort of Disgusting
Totally Disgusting
GROSS-O-METER

Sort of Disgusting
Totally Disgusting
GROSS-O-METER

The **corpse** flower is the king of smelly plants! It spends years gathering energy. Then, it releases the stench of dead bodies when it finally blooms. This huge stink bomb can grow up to 12 feet (3.6 meters) tall.

COME AND GET IT!

Flies and beetles come running when the corpse flower opens. They can smell it from more than 0.5 miles (0.8 kilometers) away!

BIG EATERS

Some hungry plants want more than rain and sunlight. The Venus flytrap waits for **prey** with open leaves. A fly lands to slurp up its **nectar**. Snap! The flytrap's leaves close tightly. It releases juices to **digest** the fly.

Sort of Disgusting
Totally Disgusting
GROSS-O-METER

Sort of Disgusting
Totally Disgusting
GROSS-O-METER

IT'S A TRAP!

The biggest pitcher plants have even been known to catch mice!

Thirsty? Do not drink out of this plant. The pitcher plant holds sweet-smelling nectar. **Insects** fly in for a sip. The slick walls keep them trapped in the juice. Slowly the juice eats away at the bugs.

DISGUSTING AND DANGEROUS

Some plants protect themselves in disgusting ways. Watch out for the manchineel tree. This tree oozes a milky **sap** that burns the skin. Smoke from burning the tree can even cause blindness.

DANGER
Fruit from the
Manchineel Tree is
Poisonous.
Handling leaves and fruit may
irritate skin and eyes
Sort of Disgusting
Totally Disgusting
GROSS-O-METER

TALL TERROR

This dangerous weed grows up to 20 feet (6 meters) high!

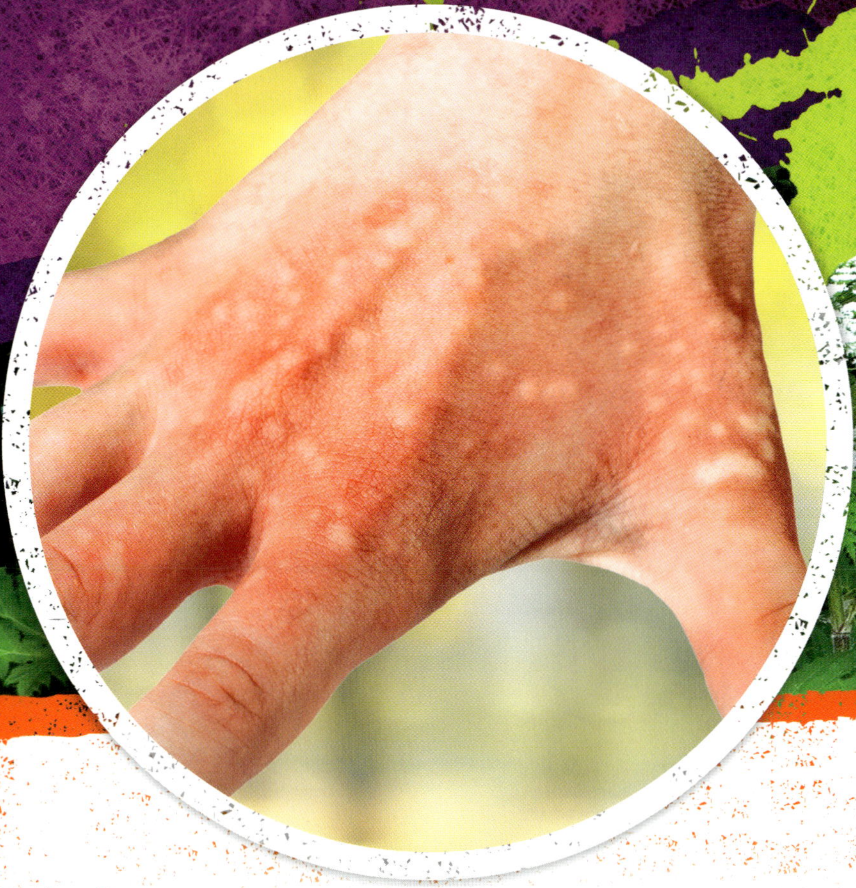

The giant hogweed looks harmless. But its sap causes horrible burns and blisters. It is one disgusting plant!

GLOSSARY

carrion—the rotting meat of dead animals

corpse—a dead body

digest—to break food down

dung—animal poop

insects—small animals with six legs and hard outer bodies; an insect's body is divided into three parts.

nectar—a sweet-tasting liquid made by plants

odor—smells; some plants use odors to attract animals.

parasite—an organism that lives by feeding off another

prey—an animal that is eaten for food

rotting—decomposing or falling apart

sap—juices that flow in a plant

TO LEARN MORE

At the Library

Batten, Mary. *Hungry Plants.* New York, N.Y.: Golden Books, 2000.

Halpern, Monica. *Venus Flytraps, Bladderworts, and Other Wild and Amazing Plants.* Washington, D.C.: National Geographic, 2006.

Lawrence, Ellen. *Freaky Plant Facts: Extreme Greens.* New York, N.Y.: Bearport Pub., 2013.

On the Web

Learning more about disgusting plants is as easy as 1, 2, 3.

1. Go to www.factsurfer.com.
2. Enter "disgusting plants" into the search box.
3. Click the "Surf" button and you will see a list of related web sites.

With factsurfer.com, finding more information is just a click away.

INDEX

The images in this book are reproduced through the courtesy of: nico99, front cover (top left); PhotoWeges, front cover (top right); kkaplin, front cover (bottom right), Scholastic cover (bottom right); iofoto, front cover (bottom left), Scholastic cover (bottom left); Horst Petzold, pp. 4-5; Cathy Keifer, pp. 5 (top right), 15; Elena Mirage, p. 5 (middle right); MongPro, p. 5 (bottom right); TfoxFoto, p. 6; NatureDiver, p. 7; Chris Mattison/ Nature Picture Library, pp. 8-9; Fadil/ Corbis, pp. 10-11; Harold Cunningham/ Getty Images, pp. 12-13; Reinhold Leitner, p. 14 (top); Mihai-Bogdan Lazar, p. 14 (bottom); Ling Kuok Loung, p. 16; Crisis2000, p. 17; Wildlife GmbH/ Alamy, pp. 18-19; yevgeniy11, p. 19; Eye Ubiquitous/ SuperStock, pp. 20-21.